D0833708

the little book of emoji insults

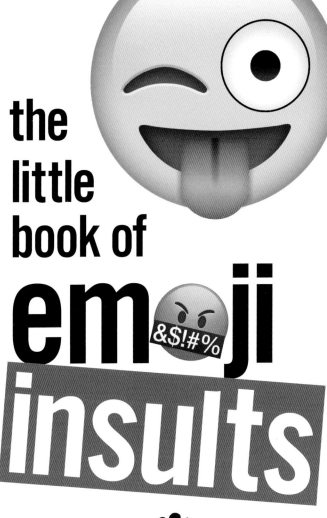

the little book of em&$!#% ji insults

POP PRESS

1 3 5 7 9 10 8 6 4 2

Pop Press, an imprint of Ebury Publishing
20 Vauxhall Bridge Road
London SW1V 2SA

Pop Press is part of the Penguin Random House group of companies
whose addresses can be found at global.penguinrandomhouse.com

Penguin
Random House
UK

Copyright © Pop Press 2018

First published by Pop Press in 2018

www.penguin.co.uk

A CIP catalogue record for this book is available from the British Library

ISBN 9781785039164

Printed and bound in China by Toppan Leefung

MIX
Paper from
responsible sources
FSC® C018179

Contents

Everyday Insults

Dumb as a doornail.

Not my cup of tea.

You bore me to tears.

Pillock.

You're as exciting as watching paint dry.

8

Beggars can't be choosers.

Read it and weep.

Clown.

Swine!

Suck it up.

9

Pinhead.

Son of a bitch.

No way, José.

You do my head in.

The black sheep of the family.

10

A pain in the ass.

Cry me a river.

Take a chill pill.

Scaredy cat!

Tell someone who gives a shit.

11

As mad as a box of frogs.

You're bananas.

Featherbrain.

Screw up.

How many times do I have flush before you'll go away?

Keep talking. One day you'll say something intelligent.

Airhead.

Boob.

You dope!

You're proof that God has a sense of humour.

13

Wanker.

Horn dog.

I've seen people like you, but I had to pay admission.

Deadbeat.

Gone to the dogs.

14

If you're going to be two-faced, at least make one face pretty.

Creep.

Sap.

Shock me – say something intelligent.

Are your parents siblings?

15

Asscake.

White trash.

A few clowns short of a circus.

Keep talking – I always yawn when I'm interested.

Dumbbell.

16

Cow.

Muttonhead.

Out to lunch.

Bonehead.

Ass wipe.

17

If ignorance is bliss, you must be the happiest person on earth.

Wank face.

Meathead.

Village idiot.

Dipstick.

Childish Taunts

Did you say something or was that the wind?

You suck.

Talk to the hand because the face ain't listening.

Your mum.

Kiss my ass.

Piece of crap.

Peabrain.

Go duck yourself.

Fat head.

Weiner.

Idiot.

Fool.

Go piss into the wind.

You look good ... NOT.

Shit for brains.

Butthole.

You smell!

Poo face.

Dicksplat.

You're dumber than snake gloves.

Bus wanker.

Eat some make-up so you can be pretty on the inside.

Asshole casserole.

Teacher's pet.

I'm telling!

Go play in traffic.

Tell-tale tit.

Liar liar pants on fire.

Your face.

Lalalalala can't hear you.

You're a meanie.

I don't like you.

Ew.

I'm telling mum!

If you like it so much, why don't you marry it?

Turd-slapper.

If I wanted to hear from an asshole, I'd fart.

Cum-guzzler.

If shit was music, you'd be an orchestra.

Whorenado.

Fart-breath.

Douche canoe.

Tool.

Mouth-breather.

Ass-clown.

I believe in respect for the dead. I'd only respect you if you were dead.

Shit-grabber.

Bumfluff.

Big, stupid doo-doo-head.

Knob-jockey.

Snot-rag.

Dickweed.

You suck donkey balls.

Buttmuncher.

Extra-Special Burns

You don't sweat much for a fat guy.

Sheepshagger.

Climb out of my arse.

You started at the bottom and it's downhill from there.

If I throw you a ball, will you go away?

32

I hope you have bad sex.

Asshat.

You must have been born on the motorway – that's where most accidents happen.

Bell end.

It looks like your face caught on fire and someone tried to put it out with chopsticks.

33

I hope someone poisons your tea.

You're such a treasure. I want to bury you.

You're as sharp as a boxing glove.

I wish your dad had pulled out.

Douchebag.

Your family tree is a cactus, because everyone in it is a prick.

I don't engage in mental combat with the unarmed.

Is your ass jealous of the shit that just came out of your mouth?

A thought crossed your mind? Must have been a lovely journey.

I wish you'd either die or shut up.

If laughter is the best medicine, your face must be curing the world.

I'd like to see things from your point of view, but I can't get my head that far up my ass.

The only way you'll get laid is if you crawl up a chicken's ass and wait.

36

Two wrongs don't make a right. Take your parents as an example.

What language are you speaking? It sounds like bullshit.

You are proof that evolution can go in reverse.

You have something on your chin ... no, on the third one.

37

If I had a face like yours, I'd sue my parents.

Stupidity is not a crime, so you're free to go.

I would give you a nasty look, but you already have one.

You are living proof that manure can sprout legs and walk.

You have the perfect face for radio.

You look like a 'before picture'.

I would ask how old you are, but I know you can't count that high.

Brains aren't everything. In your case they're nothing.

Ah, I see the Fuck-Up Fairy has visited us again.

We all sprang from apes. In your case,not far enough.

You do realise make-up won't fix your stupidity?

Hell is papered with your deleted selfies.

Your Mum

When your mum dropped you off at school, the police arrested her for littering.

Your mum's so fat, she brought a spoon to the Super Bowl.

Your mum's teeth are so yellow, when she smiled at traffic, it slowed down.

Your mum's so stupid, when she saw the 'Statue of Liberty left' sign, she went home.

Your mum's so fat, the aliens call her 'the mothership'.

Your mum's so fat, I took a picture of her last Christmas and it's still printing.

Your mum's so stupid, she stuck a battery up her ass and said, 'I GOT THE POWER!'

Your mum's so ugly, when she took a bath the water jumped out.

Your mum's so stupid, she smashed a glass door to see what was on the other side.

Your mum's so stupid, she took a ruler to bed to see how long she slept.

Your mum's so stupid, she sits on the TV and watches the couch.

Your mum's so ugly, they filmed *Gorillas in the Mist* in her shower.

Your mum's so ugly, when she walks into a bank, they turn off the surveillance cameras.

Your mum's so ugly, I heard your dad first met her at the pound.

Your mum's so fat, when she went to the beach, all the whales started singing, 'We are family'.

Your mum's so old, her breast milk is actually powder.

Your mum's so fat, she has to wear six watches for each time zone.

Your mum's so stupid, she went to the dentist to get Bluetooth.

Your mum's so dumb, when they said it was chilly outside, she grabbed a bowl.

Your mum's so fat, her Patronus is cake.

Your mum's so fat, she could sell shade.

Your mum's so ugly, she scared the crap out of the toilet.

Your mum's so stupid, she stares at soup cans that say 'concentrate'.

Your mum's like school in summertime. No class.

Your mum's such a bad cook, she uses the smoke alarm as a timer.

Your mum's so fat, she doesn't need the internet, because she's already world wide.

Relationship Slights

Marriage is like a hot bath. It gets cold fast.

Go to hell.

I've got no time for your bull.

Screw you.

How big?

Is your friend single?

Don't call me, I'll call you.

You looked better last night!

An elephant never forgets.

Gasbag.

I may love to shop, but I'm not buying your bullshit.

You're a snake.

Ball and chain.

Cut the crap.

Drama queen.

You make me sick.

Go fuck yourself.

Grow some balls!

You smell ... athletic.

I can lose weight, but you'll always be ugly.

You're not Mr Right.

Player.

We're better off as friends.

I need space.

You're whipped.

Your mate's much fitter.

It's not you, it's me.

I'm not looking for anything serious ...

 ...

We're just at different points in our lives.

The timing isn't right.

56

Friend-zoned.

What would you call a woman who goes out with you? Desperate.

No, those jeans don't make you look fatter. How could they?

Is it hot in here? Or is this relationship suffocating me?

57

Do you believe in love at first sight? How about misery after three years?

It's not you ... it's your taste in music.

My phone battery lasts longer than your relationships.

Snubs from Movies

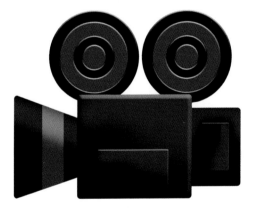

'Boo, you whore.'

Regina George to Karen Smith in *Mean Girls*

'You're just a virgin who can't drive.'

Tai Frasier to Cher Horowitz in *Clueless*

'You are a smelly pirate hooker ... Why don't you go back to your home on Whore Island?'

Ron Burgundy to Veronica Corningstone in *Anchorman*

60

'You're literally too stupid to insult.'

Stu to Alan in *The Hangover*

'Laugh it up, fuzzball.' Han Solo to Chewbacca in
Star Wars Episode V: The Empire Strikes Back

'Who took the jam out of your doughnut?'

Tommy to Turkish in *Snatch*

'Stupid hobbit! We burns you up!' Gollum to Samwise
Gamgee in *The Lord of the Rings: The Return of the King*

61

'I fart in your general direction! Your mother was a hamster and your father smelt of elderberries!'
French Soldier to King Arthur in *Monty Python and the Holy Grail*

'If you cut off her hair, she'd look like a British man.' Cady Heron on Regina George in *Mean Girls*

'At least I'm pretty enough to be a stripper. You obviously can't be a stripper. You're too ugly.'
Thirteen-year-old girl in jewellery store to Annie Walker in *Bridesmaids* (extended scene)

62

'You shut your mouth when you're talking to me!' Mrs Kroeger to Mr Kroeger in *Wedding Crashers*

'If I wanted a joke, I'd follow you into the John and watch you take a leak.'
Neal to Cab Dispatcher in *Planes, Trains and Automobiles*

'You meat-headed shit-sack.' Bill 'The Butcher' Cutting to Happy Jack Mulraney in *Gangs of New York*

'Your soul is dogshit.' Marcus to Willie in *Bad Santa*

63

'You are nothing! If you were in my toilet, I wouldn't bother flushing it.'

Buddy Ackerman to Guy in *Swimming with Sharks*

'You're not even interesting enough to make me sick.' Alexandra Medford to Daryl Van Horne in *The Witches of Eastwick*

'You warthog-faced buffoon.'

Prince Humperdinck to Westley in *The Princess Bride*

'She made out with a hot dog.'

Karen Smith of Amber D'Alessio in *Mean Girls*

64

'You are a sad, strange little man, and you have my pity.' Buzz Lightyear to Woody in *Toy Story*

'Penis-breath!' Elliott to Michael in *E.T. the Extra-Terrestrial*

'Even if I were blind, desperate, starved and begging for it on a desert island, you would be the last thing I'd ever fuck.'

Elvira Hancock to Tony Montana in *Scarface*

65

'Call me when your boobs come in.' Annie Walker to 13-year-old girl in jewellery store in *Bridesmaids*

'You sons of a motherless goat!'
Lucky Day to the Banditos in *Three Amigos*

'Your mom's chest hair.'
Janis Ian to random guy in *Mean Girls*

'I swear, I'm so pissed off at my mom. As soon as she's of age, I'm putting her in a home.'
Brennan Huff on his mom in *Step Brothers*

66

'When I watch you eat. When I see you asleep. When I look at you lately, I just want to smash your face in.'
Barbara Rose to Oliver Rose in *The War of the Roses*

'You are about the worst tourist in the whole world.' Ken to Ray in *In Bruges*

'You think you like me? You ain't like me, motherfucker. You a punk.'
Carlito to Benny Blanco in *Carlito's Way*

67

'Eat it till ya choke, you sick, twisted fuck!'

Paul Sheldon to Annie Wilkes in *Misery*

'You can walk home, bitches.'

Regina George to the girls in *Mean Girls*

'I'm going to punch you in the ovary.'

Ron Burgundy to Veronica Corningstone in *Anchorman*

Slams from TV

'Who's the bitch now?'

Jesse Pinkman to Tuco Salamanca in *Breaking Bad*

'Mother dick.'

Abraham Ford to the walkers in *The Walking Dead*

'Here's a phone. Call somebody who cares.'

Mr Burns to Lisa Simpson in *The Simpsons*

'Why don't you shut your moustache?'

Leslie Knope to Ron Swanson in *Parks and Recreation*

'Highly illogical.' Spock to everyone in *Star Trek*

70

'Come here, you senile old parasite.'
Derek Trotter to Uncle Albert in *Only Fools and Horses*

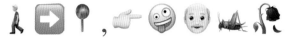

'You look like a blood donor who couldn't say
no.' Derek Trotter to Rodney Trotter in *Only Fools and Horses*

'You've had more dogs than Crufts.'
Del Boy to Rodney in *Only Fools and Horses*

'I'm fed up with you, you rancorous, coiffured
old sow. Why don't you syringe the donuts out
of your ear?' Basil Fawlty to Sybil Fawlty in *Fawlty Towers*

71

'Fuck you! And your eyebrows!'
Walter White to the car-wash boss in *Breaking Bad*

'Everything looks and sounds like shit to you.
It's a condition called "Being A Cynical
Asshole"' Doctor to Stan in *South Park*

'You're my free pass, bitch.'
Jesse Pinkman to Walter White in *Breaking Bad*

'Your tears are so yummy and sweet.'
Eric Cartman to Scott Tenorman in *South Park*

72

'Bloody, bollocky, selfish, two-faced chicken bastard, pig-dog-man.' Patsy Stone on Saffron Monsoon's dad, Justin, in *Absolutely Fabulous*

'Well, I'd love to stay and chat, but you're a total bitch.' Stewie Griffin to Olivia in *Family Guy*

'I will kill your wife, I will kill your son, I will kill your infant daughter.'
Gus Fring to Walter White in *Breaking Bad*

'You are truly the Picasso of loneliness.'
Jack Donaghy to Liz Lemon in *30 Rock*

'Good bye forever, you factory reject dildos.'
Jenna Maroney to the staff in *30 Rock*

'You look like a bird who swallowed a plate.'
Blackadder to Baldrick in *Blackadder II*

'Get bent.' Bart Simpson to everyone in *The Simpsons*

74

'Your head is as empty as a eunuch's underpants.'
Edmund Blackadder to Baldrick in *Blackadder: The Cavalier Years*

'I've seen pictures of your mother. Keep eating.'
Sheldon Cooper to Penny Hofstadter in *The Big Bang Theory*

'I'm given to understand your mother is overweight.'
Sheldon Cooper to Barry Kripke in *The Big Bang Theory*

'Suck my balls.' Eric Cartman to everyone in *South Park*

75

'In my experience with buttfaces, you are one.'

Leslie Knope to Ron Swanson in *Parks and Recreation*

'Oh, you little bitch troll from Hell.'

Patsy Stone to Saffron Monsoon in *Absolutely Fabulous*

'Bitch nuts.' Abraham Ford to the walkers in *The Walking Dead*

'Maybe you're Costa Rican. That's why your family's so poor.'

Eric Cartman to Kenny McCormick in *South Park*

'Ooo, she's so cold, sweetie! I'll just bet she has her periods in cubes.'

Patsy Stone of Saffron Monsoon in *Absolutely Fabulous*

'I'm going to set your face on fire.'

Dwight Schrute to Jim Halpert in *The Office* (US)

'You're so white.'

Michael Scott to Toby Flenderson in *The Office* (US)

'The shit you cook is shit.'

Walter White to Jesse Pinkman in *Breaking Bad*

77

'How are you not murdered every hour?'
Andy Bernard to Toby Flenderson in *The Office* (US)

'I'm going to make you my prison bitch ...
I'm going to make you my house mouse.'
Piper Chapman to Dina in *Orange is the New Black*

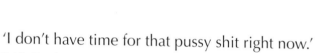

'I don't have time for that pussy shit right now.'
Pablo Escobar on the phone in *Narcos*

'Gonorrhoea bastard son of a bitch.'
Pablo Escobar to Horacio Carrillo in *Narcos*

78

'He's as slimy as a hagfish, with none of the charm.' Steve Murphy about Alberto Suarez in *Narcos*

'Don't "but" me, you little snot rag!'
Patsy Stone to the intern in *Absolutely Fabulous*

'You better watch your mouth, sunshine.'
Daryl Dixon to Milton Mamet in *The Walking Dead*

'Your baby isn't even that cute.'
Amy Green to Rachel Green in *Friends*

the little book of emoji insults slams from tv

79

'I'd laugh in your face but I'm saving my voice.'
Niles Crane to Frasier Crane in *Frasier*

'Don't talk out loud. You lower the IQ of the whole street.' Sherlock Holmes to Philip Anderson in *Sherlock*

'You two suck at peddling meth.' Saul Goodman to Walter White and Jesse Pinkman in *Breaking Bad*

'Planet of the pudding brains.'
Doctor Who on the Earth in *Doctor Who*

'You're like a sweaty octopus trying to unhook a bra.' Malcolm Tucker to Ben Swain in *The Thick of It*

'There's no cure for being a cunt.'
Bronn on Joffrey Baratheon in *Game of Thrones*

Song Disses

'I know you like to think your shit don't stink, but lean a little bit closer and see that roses really smell like oooh-ooh-ooh.' OutKast, 'Roses'

'If your boyfriend says he got beef, well, I'm a vegetarian and I ain't fucking scared of him.'
3OH!3, 'Don't Trust Me'

'That's no problem, problem, problem, the problem is you.' The Sex Pistols, 'Problems'

'Who do you think you are? Some kind of superstar?' Spice Girls, 'Who Do You Think You Are?'

'Read a book, you illiterate son of a bitch, and pick up your vocab.' Jay-Z, 'Big Pimpin''

'You're an idiot, babe. It's a wonder that you still know how to breathe.' Bob Dylan, 'Idiot Wind'

'Talking like a queen, when you looking like a lab rat.' Nicki Minaj, 'Stupid Hoe'

'If I never see your face again, I don't mind.'

Maroon 5, 'If I Never See Your Face Again'

'I got 99 problems, but a bitch ain't one.'

Jay-Z, '99 Problems'

'It's too late and I can't wait for you to be gone.'

Jojo, 'Leave (Get Out)'

'The bridge has been burned, now it's your turn to cry.' Justin Timberlake, 'Cry Me a River'

85

'You're a bum, you're a punk, you're an old slut on junk.' The Pogues, 'Fairytale of New York'

'You got mud on your face, you big disgrace, kicking your can all over the place.'
Queen, 'We Will Rock You'

'How do you sleep at night?'
John Lennon, 'How Do You Sleep?'

'You need to act your age and not your girl's age.' Drake, '6pm in New York'

'You're a spineless, pale, pathetic lot, and you haven't got a clue.' 'I'll Make a Man Out of You', from *Mulan*

'Man try say he's better than me. Tell my man shut up.' Stormzy, 'Shut Up'

'Bout to call your ass an Uber, I got somewhere to be.' Drake, 'Energy'

'Go 'head and sell me out and I'll lay your shit bare.' Adele, 'Rolling in the Deep'

'You ain't nothing but a hound dog, cryin' all the time. Well, you ain't never caught a rabbit and you ain't no friend of mine.' Elvis Presley, 'Hound Dog'

'Acting up, drink in my cup, I can't care less what you think.' Beyoncé, 'Single Ladies (Put a Ring on It)'

'My milkshake bring all the boys to the yard. And they're like it's better than yours.' Kelis, 'Milkshake'

'Leave me alone, stop it! Just stop dogging me around.' Michael Jackson, 'Leave Me Alone'

'Honey, I rose up from the dead, I do it all the time. I've got a list of names and yours is in red, underlined.' Taylor Swift, 'Look What You Made Me Do'

'I'm looking like class, and he's looking like trash. Can't get with a deadbeat ass.' TLC, 'No Scrubs'

'You made a really deep cut and, baby, now we have bad blood.' Taylor Swift, 'Bad Blood'

'At first when I see you cry, yeah, it makes me smile.' Lily Allen, 'Smile'

'You ain't even lord of your yard.' Stormzy, 'Shut Up'

'Someday, I'll be living in a big ol' city, and all you're ever gonna be is mean.' Taylor Swift, 'Mean'

90

'Stop right now, thank you very much. I need somebody with a human touch.' Spice Girls, 'Stop'

'I don't like your little games, don't like your tilted stage.' Taylor Swift, 'Look What You Made Me Do'

'But if everybody's crazy, you're the one who's insane.' Jay-Z, 'Kill Jay-Z'

'You're getting way too big for your boots.'
Stormzy, 'Big for Your Boots'

'I'm a boss, you a worker bitch. I make bloody moves.' Cardi B, 'Bodak Yellow'

'You 36-year-old, baldheaded fag, blow me! ... It's over.' Eminem, 'Without Me'

'Your reign on the top was short like leprechauns.' The Notorious B.I.G., 'Kick in the Door'

Literary Contempt

'You ride well, but you don't kiss nicely at all.'
Stephen to Elfride in *A Pair of Blue Eyes* by Thomas Hardy

'I am not interested in emotional fuckwittage.
Goodbye.' Bridget Jones to Daniel Cleaver in *Bridget Jones's Diary* by Helen Fielding

'You are the last man in the world I could ever
be prevailed upon to marry.' Elizabeth Bennet to
Mr Darcy in *Pride and Prejudice* by Jane Austen

'As useless as nipples on a breastplate.'
Cersei Lannister of the Kingsguard Knights in *A Song of Ice and Fire, A Dance with Dragons*

94

'A prig is a fellow who is always making you a present of his opinions.'

Fred Vincy of Tertius Lydgate in *Middlemarch* by George Eliot

'My dear, I don't give a damn.' Rhett Butler to Scarlett O'Hara in *Gone with the Wind* by Margaret Mitchell

'Eat my shit.'

Minny to Hilly Holbrook in *The Help* by Kathryn Stockett

'If you will forgive me for being personal – I don't like your face.' Hercule Poirot to Mr Ratchett in *Murder on the Orient Express* by Agatha Christie

95

'May your genitals sprout wings and fly away.'
Om-as-Tortoise curse on Brother Nhumrod in *Small Gods* by
Terry Pratchett

'How art thou, thou globby bottle of cheap,
stinking chip-oil?'
Alex to Billyboy in *A Clockwork Orange* by Anthony Burgess

'He was simply a hole in the air.' George Orwell on
Stanley Baldwin in 'The Lion and the Unicorn'

'She is nuttier than squirrel poo.'
Enid Smeek on Bathilda Bagshot in *Harry Potter and the Deathy
Hallows* by J.K. Rowling

96

'If your brains were dynamite there wouldn't be enough to blow your hat off.' Kilgore Trout to anyone he doesn't like in *Timequake* by Kurt Vonnegut

'Keep runnin' that mouth of yours ... I'm gonna take you in the back and screw you.' Llewelyn Moss to Carla Jean Moss in *No Country for Old Men* by Cormac McCarthy

'I wolde I hadde thy coillons in myn hond ... Lat kutte hem off.' (I wish I had your balls in my hand ... Let's cut 'em off.') The Host to the Pardoner in *The Canterbury Tales* by Geoffrey Chaucer

97

'I never saw anybody take so long to dress, and with such little result.' Algernon Moncrieff to Jack Worthing in *The Importance of Being Earnest* by Oscar Wilde

'It should take you about four seconds from here to the door. I'll give you two.'

Truman Capote, *Breakfast at Tiffany's*

'Your hair wants cutting.'

The Mad Hatter to Alice in *Alice in Wonderland* by Lewis Carroll

'A crrritic!'

Estragon to Vladmir in *Waiting for Godot* by Samuel Beckett

'He would make a lovely corpse.'
Mrs Gamp of a young man in *The Life and Adventures of Martin Chuzzlewit* by Charles Dickens

'You fleabitten fungus! You bursting blister! You moth-eaten maggot!'
Mrs Trunchbull to Wilfred in *Matilda* by Roald Dahl

'You see, but you do not observe.' Sherlock Holmes to Dr Watson in *A Scandal in Bohemia* by Arthur Conan Doyle

'What are you now? A third-rate actress with a pretty face.' Dorian Gray to Sibyl Vane in *The Picture of Dorian Gray* by Oscar Wilde

99

'What a pair of frauds.'

Mike Engleby of his interviewers in *Engleby* by Sebastian Faulks

'There's a stake in your fat black heart.
And the villagers never liked you.'

Sylvia Plath to her father in 'Daddy'

'Bitch. You rich bitch.' Harry to Helen in 'The Snows of
Kilimanjaro' by Ernest Hemingway

'Why do you sit there looking like an envelope
without any address on it?' Sally Sellers to Howard
Tracy in *The American Claimant* by Mark Twain

Shakespeare's Zingers

'Villain, I have done thy mother.'

Aaron to Chiron in *Titus Andronicus*

'A most notable coward.'

Second Lord of Parolles in *All's Well that Ends Well*

'Away, you three-inch fool!'

Curtis to Grumio in *The Taming of the Shrew*

'More of your conversation would infect my brain.'

Menenius to Brutus and Sicinius in *Coriolanus*

'Peace, ye fat-guts!'
Henry V to Falstaff in *Henry IV, Part I*

'Such bugs and goblins in my life.'
Hamlet of Rosencrantz and Guildenstern in *Hamlet*

'The rankest compound of villainous smell that ever offended nostril.'
Falstaff to Ford in *The Merry Wives of Windsor*

'Her beauty and her brain go not together.'
First Lord of Cymbeline in *Cymbeline*

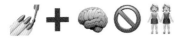

103

'I am sick when I do look on thee.'
Demetrius to Helena in *A Midsummer Night's Dream*

'I was seeking for a fool when I found you.'
Jacques to Orlando in *As You Like It*

'This woman's an easy glove; she goes off and on at pleasure.'
Lafeu of Diana in *All's Well that Ends Well*

'There's neither honesty, manhood, nor good fellowship in thee.'
Falstaff to Prince Henry in *Henry IV, Part I*

'Thou elvish-mark'd, rooting hog!'
Queen Margaret to Richard in *Richard III*

'Thou damned and luxurious mountain goat.'
Pistol to French Soldier in *Henry V*

'The tartness of his face sours ripe grapes.'
Menenius of Marcius in *Coriolanus*

'I do desire that we be better strangers.'
Orlando to Jacques in *As You Like It*

'His beastly mind.'

Imogen of Iachimo in *Cymbeline*

'You mad-headed ape!'

Lady Percy to Hotspur in *Henry IV, Part I*

'Wedded be thou to the hags of hell.'

Captain to the Earl of Suffolk in *Henry VI, Part II*

'Thy detestable bones.'

Constance to King Philip in *King John*

'False of heart, light of ear, bloody of hand; hog in sloth, fox in stealth, wolf in greediness, dog in madness, lion in prey.' Edgar of himself in *King Lear*

'Weed this wormwood from your fruitful brain.'
Rosaline to Berowne in *Love's Labours' Lost*

'You should be women, and yet your beards forbid me to interpret that you are so.'
Macbeth to the witches in *Macbeth*

'Thou paper-fac'd villain.'
Doll Tearsheet to Beadle in *Henry IV, Part II*

'I'll pray a thousand prayers for thy death.'
Isabella to Claudio in *Measure for Measure*

'You'll surely sup in hell.'
Richard to Young Clifford in *Henry VI, Part II*

'A plague o' both your houses!'
Tybalt to the Montagues and Capulets in *Romeo and Juliet*

'Art thou lunatics?'
Eva to William and Quickly in *The Merry Wives of Windsor*

'Toads, beetles, bats, light on you!'
Caliban to Prospero in *The Tempest*

'You secret, black and midnight hags.'
Macbeth to the witches in *Macbeth*

'I do repent the tedious minutes I with her have spent.'
Lysander of Hermia in *A Midsummer Night's Dream*

'A monster, a very monster in apparel.'
Biondello of Grumio in *The Taming of the Shrew*

'I noted her not, but I looked on her.'
Benedick of Hero in *Much Ado About Nothing*

'You rise to play, and go to bed to work.'
Iago of women in *Othello*

'Out of my sight! Thou dost infect mine eyes.'
Anne to Richard in *Richard III*

'You ratcatcher.'

Mercutio to Tybalt in *Romeo and Juliet*

'Do thou amend thy face.'

Falstaff to Bardolph in *Henry IV, Part I*

'If he be sad, he wants money.'

Don Pedro of Benedick in *Much Ado About Nothing*

'There's small choice in rotten apples.'

Hortensio of Katherina in *The Taming of the Shrew*

'Hell is empty, and all the devils are here.'
Ferdinand in peril, in *The Tempest*

'I will bite my thumb at them.'
Sampson of the Montagues in *Romeo and Juliet*

'You tread upon my patience.'
King Henry to Worchester in *Henry IV, Part I*

'Neighbours, you are tedious.'
Leonato of Dogberry and Verges in *Much Ado About Nothing*

112

Putdowns in Sport

'You are a fucking wanker and you can stick your World Cup up your arse.'
Roy Keane to Mick McCarthy

'The Rock gets more pie in one night than you get in a lifetime.' The Rock's catchphrase

'Why are you so fat?'
'Because everytime I make love to your wife, she gives me a biscuit.'
Eddo Brandes in response to Glen McGrath

114

'That lad must have been born offside.'
Alex Ferguson on Filippo Inzaghi

'He's boring, isn't he?' Freddy Shepherd on Alan Shearer

'A bunch of nerds.' Joey Porter on the Indianapolis Colts

'He likes to watch other people. There are some guys who, when they are at home, have a big telescope to see what happens in other families.' José Mourinho on Arsène Wenger

115

'Look into my eyes, little man. You're going to die.' Connor McGregor to José Aldo

'The Rock knows that you got one eye that goes that way, and another eye that goes that way.'
The Rock to Triple H

'He's too ugly to be world champion.'
Muhammad Ali on Sonny Liston

'Answer the question! The question, jerk!'
John McEnroe to an umpire during the match.

116

'I would prefer the whore that is your sister.'

Marco Materazzi to Zinedine Zidane

'A midget, German steroid head.'

Connor McGregor on Dennis Siver

'Float like a butterfly, sting like a bee. His hands can't hit what his eyes can't see.'

Muhammad Ali on George Foreman

'The Rock will check you directly into the SmackDown Hotel.' The Rock's catchphrase

117

'He cannot kick with his left foot, he cannot head a ball, he cannot tackle and he doesn't score many goals. Apart from that he's all right.' George Best on David Beckham

'He should go back to the museum.'
Diego Maradona on Pelé

'Tell him I'm his daddy. Sit on my lap kid.'
Connor McGregor to José Aldo

118

'You won, but I'm prettier and more marketable than you.' Anna Kournikova to Martina Hingis

'You'll be sorry you hit me, you fucking communist ass.' John McEnroe to Tomáš Šmíd

'Shut up. Grow up. You're a baby. I've got a son your age.' Jimmy Connors to John McEnroe

'I'll take a bath in his blood.'
Mike Tyson on Francois Botha

119

'More robotic than a parrot.'

Andre Agassi on Pete Sampras

'Know your role and shut your mouth.'

The Rock's catchphrase

'You're a liar ... You're a fucking wanker.'

Roy Keane to Mick McCarthy

'His wife can't sing and his barber can't cut hair.' Brian Clough on David Beckham

120

'He will never be anything more than a water carrier.' Eric Cantona on Didier Deschamps

'The left side of your head is drooping. I'm worried, I'm honestly worried. I love you, I love you like my little bitch.' Connor McGregor on José Aldo

'A specialist in failure.' José Mourinho on Arsène Wenger

'I'm not as nice as all that. In fact, I swore only last week.' Gary Lineker on himself

121

Celebs Getting Mean

'My gran could do it better and she's dead.'

Gordon Ramsay to a contestant

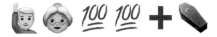

'I'm tempted to know if you sang that the night before your wife left you.'

Simon Cowell to a contestant

'You can put lipstick on a pig ... it's still a pig.'

Barack Obama dig at Sarah Palin

'She looks like a fairground stripper'

Elton John on Madonna

123

'I wish you would jump in the oven.'

Gordon Ramsay to a contestant

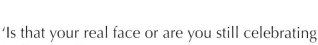

'Is that your real face or are you still celebrating Halloween?' Arthur Smith to a heckler

'A beached whale.' Lord Sugar on Piers Morgan

'Your bus leaves in 10 minutes ... Be under it.'

John Cooper Clarke to a heckler

'What are you? An idiot sandwich?'

Gordon Ramsay to a contestant

124

'You've just invented a new form of torture.'
Simon Cowell to a contestant

'Why don't you go into that corner and finish evolving?' Russell Kane to a heckler

'You fucking donkey.' Gordon Ramsay to a contestant

'When they put teeth in your mouth, they spoiled a perfectly good bum.' Billy Connolly to a heckler

'She looks like a boiled horse.'
Jeremy Clarkson on Sarah Jessica Parker

'You're so old, when you were born rainbows were black and white.' Will Ferrell to Mark Wahlberg

'You're not a nice person.' Mark Wahlberg to Will Ferrell

'There's no beginning to your talents ...'
Clive Anderson to Jeffrey Archer

'Little rocket man.' Donald Trump on Kim Jong-un

'A deranged US dotard.' Kim Jong-un on Donald Trump

126

'You sounded like three cats being dragged up the motorway.' Simon Cowell to three contestants

'OK, your conversations are too long bye.'
Kourtney Kardashian to Kris Jenner

'A giant orange Twitter egg.'
J.K. Rowling on Donald Trump

'Your voice sounds like a girl crying. Everytime you speak, do you give yourself an erection?'
Amy Schumer to a heckler

'If she was your girlfriend, she was probably blind.' James Blunt to a Twitter troll

'If she wants us to see a part of her we've never seen, she's gonna have to swallow the camera'
Bette Midler on Kim Kardashian

'It was like ordering a hamburger and only getting the bun.' Simon Cowell to a contestant